The List

The List

A Love Story

in 781

Chapters

by Aneva Stout

Illustrations by Maggie Stewart

WORKMAN PUBLISHING ♥ **NEW YORK**

For Octavia

IN MEMORY OF MY MOM AND DAD

Library of Congress Cataloguing-in-Publication Data is available.

Workman books are available at special discounts when purchased in
bulk for premiums and sales promotions as well as for fund-raising or
educational use. Special editions can also be created to specification.
For details, contact the Special Sales Director at the address below.

Designed by Janet Vicario with Ellen Korbonski

WORKMAN PUBLISHING COMPANY, INC.
708 Broadway
New York, NY 10003-9555
www.workman.com

Printed in Mexico

First Printing: March 2006

10 9 8 7 6 5 4 3 2 1

Acknowledgments

Love and thanks to Carol Beirne, Nancy McLaughlin, John Harriman, Helen Lindley, Robert Johnson, Marcie Shepard, Carolynn Mowen, and Victor Nunez for believing in me long enough to write a book.

A special thanks to my dear friends Nerissa Nelson and Jeff Marks, who tolerated my nonsense ("You don't care what color the cat is? Just wait until *you* need help!"), encouraged me with dinner promises, and made writing this book possible because of their love and support.

To my coworkers, Tanya Bartule, Lauren Titlebaum, and Carlos Cortes, whose constant harassment ("Are you finished yet?") was needed more than they know.

And to my editor, Susan Bolotin, for giving me one of the three happiest days of my life, and sharing her expertise with humor, kindness, and grace.

Thank you.

1. You will dream about meeting Mr. Right.
   a. You'll be eleven.
   b. Twelve.
   c. Forty-six.

2. Your first Mr. Right will be a rock star.

3. Your first Mr. Wrong will be a musician.

4. You will not learn from this.

5. You will get advice about men from your mother.
   a. "It's as easy to love a rich man as a poor man."
   b. "The way to a man's heart is through his stomach."
   c. "Good luck."

6. You'll decide your mother has no idea what she's talking about.
   a. Until you're her age.

7. You'll go out with a girlfriend, hoping to meet Mr. Right.
   a. You'll be twenty.
   b. Thirty.
   c. Your mother's age.

8. You'll meet a man in a bar.

   a. The bartender.

   b. The bouncer.

   c. A banker.

   d. A man who's wearing a T-shirt that says: Eat Me.

9. You'll go out with the banker.

10. He'll ask you if you ever watch CNN.

11. He'll ask you if you own any mutual funds.

12. He'll order a virgin margarita.

   a. No salt.

13. You'll need a tequila.

14. You'll wish you had picked the guy who was wearing a T-shirt that said: *Eat Me*.

15. You'll go out with a guy who looks like he might own a T-shirt that says: *Eat Me*.

16. He'll ask you if you've ever seen *Spider-Man*.

17. He'll ask you if you have any money because he forgot his.

18. He'll ask you if he can borrow some money until he gets paid.

19. You'll go home and call your mother.

20. You'll go home and eat a pint of Häagen-Dazs.

21. You'll go home and call your ex.

22. A woman will answer the phone.

23. She'll have a French accent.

24. You'll break out the vodka.

25. And call your ex again.

26. You'll leave a message on his answering machine.

27. You'll barely remember the message in the morning.

28. Your ex will never forget it.

29. His French girlfriend will never forget it.
  a. It will remind her of the drunken message she left her ex.

30. You'll tell yourself you'll never call a man when you're drunk.
  a. Ha.

31. You'll call your girlfriend and say, "You're never going to believe what I did last night."

32. She'll say, "You got drunk and called your ex."

33. You'll be grateful for your girlfriends.

34. You'll decide that you don't need a man.

35. You'll think: I have my girlfriends.
  a. I have my job.
  b. I have a cat.

36. You'll share your Häagen-Dazs with your cat.

37. You'll watch a whole season of *Sex and the City.*

38. You'll sit in a café with a good book.

39. You'll wonder why you ever thought you wanted a man in your life.

40. A man seated near you in the café will ask you what you're reading.

41. He'll be tall.
   a. Dark.
   b. Handsome.
   c. French.
   d. Okay, he won't be French.

42. You'll say, *"War and Peace."*
   a. "Remembrance of Things Past."
   b. "If I'm So Wonderful, Why Am I Still Single?"

43. He'll say, "I love Tolstoy."

44. You'll wonder why you ever wondered about wanting a man in your life.

45. You'll wonder why you ever doubted that you'd meet a man.

46. You'll have an afternoon you thought could happen only in the movies.

47. You'll call your girlfriend and say, "You're never going to believe what happened to me today."

48. She'll say, "You locked your keys in the car."

49. You'll say, "No, I met someone."

50. She'll say, "Oh, God, that's worse."

51. You'll say, "Guess who he looks like."

52. She'll say, "George Clooney?"

53. You'll say, "Seriously."

54. She'll say, "Kiefer Sutherland?"

55. You'll say, "No, Liam Neeson."

56. Your girlfriend will act impressed.

57. You'll say, "Guess who his favorite author is."

58. She'll say, "Tom Clancy?"

59. You'll say, "No, Tolstoy."

60. Your girlfriend will act impressed again.

61. You'll say, "Guess what he does for a living."

62. She'll say, "He makes a living?"

63. You'll say, "Yep."

64. Your girlfriend will *be* impressed.

65. Your cat will look bored.

66. You'll tell your girlfriend that you have a date with the handsome stranger Saturday night.

67. She'll say six words to you that only a girlfriend would have the heart to say.
   a. "What are you going to wear?"

68. You'll have a one-word response.
   a. "Shit."

69. Your girlfriend will tell you that she'll be right over.

70. You'll feel grateful for your girlfriends again.

71. You'll pull everything out of your closet.

72. You'll pull everything out of your drawers.

73. You'll realize you have nothing to wear.

74. Your cat will realize that he has a new bed.

75. Your girlfriend will walk in and see your empty closet.
   a. Your empty drawers.
   b. The cat, who's never looked happier.

76. You'll say, "I know it's hard to believe, but I have nothing to wear."

77. She won't question you.

78. She won't judge you.

79. She won't be allergic to cats.

80. She'll say, "I guess we're going to have to go shopping."

81. You'll wonder why a man can't be more like a woman.

   a. This is one of life's great mysteries.

82. You'll find the perfect dress,

   a. the perfect shoes,

   b. the perfect lipstick;

   c. nail polish,

   d. perfume,

   e. Wonderbra.

83. You'll realize you can't afford to date.

84. You'll realize your feminism class was a waste of money.

85. You'll realize your money management books were a waste of money.

86. You'll make a vow to stop wasting money.

87. You'll make a vow to finish reading *The Second Sex* even though it's almost as long as *War and Peace*.

88. You'll go home and finish reading *Star* magazine: "Celebrities—Best and Worst Beach Bodies."

89. You'll obsess over your body.

90. You'll obsess over your hair.

91. You'll obsess over your weight.

92. You'll hate yourself.

93. You'll discover your favorite celebrity has cellulite.

94. You'll feel better about yourself.

95. You'll discover Uma Thurman hates herself too.

96. You'll feel even better.

97. Your cat will wonder when you're going to get your nose out of the magazine and feed him.

98. Then you'll see another article: "Ten Signs He's Mr. Right—The Stars Tell All."

99. You'll realize *Star* magazine is not a waste of money.

100. You'll scan the list to see if any of the stars say, "Drinks coffee with cream."

101. You'll remember how cute he was stirring his coffee.

102. You'll remember how deep he was talking about literature.

103. You'll remember he was tall.

104. You won't remember the last time you felt this excited about a man.

105. The phone will ring.

106. You'll be afraid to answer it.

107. You'll be afraid *not* to answer it.

108. You'll answer it.

109. It'll be your ex.

110. He'll tell you he's calling because he's worried about you.

111. You'll say, "Worried about *me*?"

112. Your cat will wander off to see if there's anything left in his food bowl.

113. You'll wonder why one ex becomes a friend for life.

114. And two others owe you money.

115. You'll hear your ex's girlfriend say, "*Mon chéri*" in the background.

116. It won't matter that *you* broke up with *him*.

117. It won't matter that you broke up four years ago.

118. It won't matter that you have a date with a handsome stranger Saturday night.
    a. Okay, it'll matter a little.

119. You'll feel jealous of your ex's new woman.

120. You'll tell your ex that you have a hot date Saturday night.

121. It won't matter to him that his girlfriend is French.
   a. Modeling to put herself through school.
   b. Writing her thesis on Simone de Beauvoir.

122. He'll feel jealous too.

123. You'll thank your ex for calling and tell him that you'll stay away from the vodka.

124. You'll make a vow to stop lying to men.

125. The handsome stranger will call.

126. He'll ask you what you're doing.

127. You'll say, "Making Swedish meatballs."
   a. "Reading Camus."
   b. "Feeding my cat."

128. He'll say, "Oh, you have a cat. What kind?"

129. You won't remember anything about your cat.

130. You won't remember your own name.

131. You'll say, "Oh, you know, the furry kind."

132. He'll say, "I love cats."

133. You will be sure that you have met Mr. Right.

134. He will have no idea who you really are.

135. You'll feel like a teenager.

136. You'll worry about getting a pimple before your first date.

137. You'll worry about the world coming to an end before your first date.

138. You'll worry about walking in front of a bus before your first date.

139. You'll read your horoscope.

140. According to the *Star* your future looks bright.

141. You'll feel much better.

142. You'll glance one more time at the celebrity with cellulite.

143. Then you'll feed your cat and apologize for forgetting he's striped.

144. You'll realize you have a couple of things to do before your big date.
 a. Shave.
 b. Pluck.
 c. Manicure.
 d. Pedicure.
 e. Highlight.
 f. Bikini wax.
 g. Scrub your tile.
 h. Polish your furniture.
 i. Change the kitty litter.

145. You'll schedule your hair appointment first.

146. You'll schedule your bikini wax before you change your mind.

147. You'll wonder if a man is worth all this.
   a. The odds are 50/50.
   b. Okay, 40/60.
   c. Okay, about the same as roulette, but you'll have fun in the meantime.

148. You'll fantasize about the romantic dinner.

149. You'll fantasize about gazing into his eyes.

150. You'll fantasize about the first kiss.

151. You'll remember you're a realist.

152. You'll remember your last boyfriend.

153. You'll remember you read *The Second Sex*.
   a. Okay, you skimmed most of it.

154. You'll tell yourself you're not going to get worked up over a man.

155. You'll tell yourself that sparkling bathroom tile is important to you.

156. You'll tell yourself that you're a strong, independent woman who does not wait by the phone for a man to call.

157. You'll wonder why he hasn't called.
   a. In the past 24 hours.

158. You'll check your messages again.

159. You'll check missed calls again.

160. You'll check the phone for a dial tone.
   a. Yep—a dial tone.

161. You'll wonder if he actually hates cats.
   a. Camus.
   b. Swedish meatballs.

162. You'll wonder if he met another woman.
   a. In the past 24 hours.
   b. A tall, blonde, Swedish woman who <u>really</u> makes Swedish meatballs.

163. You'll hate yourself again.

164. You won't care who else has cellulite.

165. You'll call your girlfriend and say, "I hate myself."

166. She'll say, "So does Uma Thurman."

167. Then she'll say, "Oh, God, he hasn't called."

168. Her words will leave you speechless.

169. Then she'll say, "Did you file a missing person's report?"

170. You'll say, "This isn't funny."

171. Then she'll say five words only a girlfriend would think to say.
  a. "Why don't you call <u>him</u>?"

172. The weight of this question will leave you speechless.

173. You'll ponder this question as planet Earth continues to rotate.

174. You'll ponder this question over a drink.

175. You'll laugh at yourself for making such a big deal about calling a man.

176. You'll think: He'd be lucky to get me.
   a. What man wouldn't want me?
   b. He isn't that cute.

177. You'll pick up the phone and call the handsome stranger.

178. You'll be lucky he isn't home.

179. You'll be lucky you only had one drink.

180. You'll hang up the phone before his answering machine beeps.

181. You'll think: My God, what was I thinking?
   a. If you can answer that question, you'll get your money back for this book.

182. You'll wonder if he has Caller ID.

183. You'll torment yourself wondering if he has Caller ID.

184. You'll understand why anyone might be worried about you.

185. Anyone would understand if you needed a second drink.

186. The phone will ring.

187. You'll pray that it's anyone but the man you were praying would call you.

188. It'll be your mother.

189. You'll realize you forgot to say: except my mother.

190. She'll tell you she's worried about you.

191. She'll tell you she can't understand why you're still single.

192. She'll tell you someone in the family is getting married.

193. She'll tell you that the groom's best man is available.

194. You'll have a second drink.

195. Then you'll fall asleep with Mr. Right. The furry kind.

196. You'll dream about being a bride.

197. The groom will be faceless.

198. The dress will be Vera Wang.

199. The ring will be Harry Winston.

200. The phone will ring again.

201. You'll wonder who the hell just woke you up from a perfect dream.

202. It'll be the handsome stranger.

203. He'll say, "I can't stop thinking about you."

204. Your life will exceed your dreams.
a. Once.

205. A man will exceed your dreams.
a. For about three weeks.

206. The handsome stranger will say, "See you Saturday night."

207. Three days will feel like three weeks.

208. Three hours will be the time you spend getting ready Saturday night.

209. Two of the three hours will be spent on hair.

210. It will all be worth it.

211. You will have a perfect first date with a man.

212. The wine will exceed your expectations.

213. The food will exceed your expectations.

214. The man will be cuter, smarter, deeper, taller than you thought the first time you met him.

215. The man will think you are smarter, deeper, blonder, bigger-chested than he remembered the first time he met you.

216. He'll gaze into your eyes.

217. You'll gaze into his.

218. You'll ignore the waiter.

219. You'll feel a deep, mysterious connection with the man.

220. You'll wonder if this feeling is love or lust.
a. Yep—lust.

221. You'll wonder if lust leads to love.
a. Nope, it just leads to sex.
b. Okay, sometimes it leads to love.

222. The handsome stranger will kiss you good night.

223. You won't care what it is.

224. You'll call your girlfriend and say, "I think I met the one."

225. She won't remind you of the last time you said this.

226. She won't remind you that according to statistics you have a better chance of getting struck by lightning than meeting Mr. Right.

227. She won't ask you if you had one drink or two.

228. She'll say, "Tell me everything."

229. You'll realize that half the fun of men is talking about them.

230. You'll realize the other half is thinking about them.

231. You'll realize that the man himself really has very little to do with anything.
   a. Unless you fall in love with him.

232. Yep, you will fall in love.
a. With Mr. Right.
b. With Mr. Wrong.
c. With a man who owns a PlayStation.

233. You will lose weight.

234. You will lose sleep.

235. You will lose whatever sense you had to begin with.

236. You will lose all sense of yourself.
a. And this is the fun part.
b. And this is what we're all hoping happens to us.

237. You'll smile on your way to work.

238. You'll giggle to yourself in public.

239. You'll call your girlfriend and say, "Can you believe I locked my keys in the car today?"
a. "Silly old me."
b. "Don't you hate when that happens?"
c. "Can you believe that happened to John/ Johnny/Jonathan once too?"

240. You'll annoy your friends.

241. You'll annoy your cat.

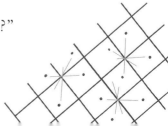

242. You'd make *yourself* sick if you could see past the tip of your nose.
a. Or the color of his eyes.
b. Or the sex.

243. You'll have the best sex of your life.
a. For about 9½ weeks.

244. It'll be worth it.

245. You'll wonder how sex could ever be so hot.

246. You'll wonder how sex could ever be so wild.

247. You'll wonder how ceramic tile could ever be so cold.

248. You'll wonder how he keeps his ceramic tile so sparkling.

249. He'll say, "Are you okay?"

250. You'll say, "Don't stop!"

251. You'll say things to your lover that you never
thought you'd hear yourself say.

   a. "You make me feel like a woman."

   b. "You complete me."

   c. "I'd like you to meet my parents."

252. You'll introduce your lover to your parents.

253. This meeting will not turn out as planned.

254. Your lover will tell your parents something you
wish he didn't.

   *a. "No, I didn't graduate. I think life is the
   greatest teacher."*

   b. "I was Jewish, but I converted to Buddhism."

   c. "What's for supper?"

255. Your parents will say something you wish they
didn't say.

   *a. "I'm glad she's finally met someone; we were
   starting to worry about her."*

   *b. "I'm glad she's finally met someone decent—
   Jeez, remember the last guy?"*

   c. "What's burning?"

256. You'll buy books you never thought you'd buy.

    a. Swedish Cuisine for Dummies.

    b. How to Please a Man.

    c. The Everything Fly-Fishing Book.

    d. Linda Goodman's Love Signs.

    e. (Okay, you probably had that one already.)

257. You'll try something you never thought
you'd try.

    a. Rafting.

    b. Snowboarding.

    c. Velveeta.

    d. (Okay, you probably tried that one already.)

258. You'll write a poem for your lover.

259. Your lover will write a poem for you.

260. You'll think he's e. e. cummings.

261. He'll play the guitar for you.

262. You'll think there's no end to the man's talents.

263. He'll get dressed in the morning.

264. You'll think there's no end to the man's talents.

265. You'll love the way he shaves.

266. You'll love the way he eats.

267. You'll love the way he drives.
   a. This will be the first to go.

268. He'll play his favorite CD for you in the car.
   a. You'll love it.
   b. You'll hate it.
   *c. You'll wonder why all men pretend the steering
       wheel is a drum set.*

269. You'll be moved by silly love songs.

270. You'll be moved by tragic love songs.

271. You'll feel tortured.

272. This, of course, will only make the sex better.

273. This, of course, will only make you feel more tortured.

    a. For some reason this inanity will make you feel alive.

    b. For some reason therapists make a lot of money.

274. You won't care about money.

275. You'll think: Who needs money when you have love?

276. You'll think: Who needs cash when you have credit?

277. You'll buy an extravagant gift for your lover.

278. You'll receive an extravagant gift from your lover.

279. You'll receive a gift that makes you wonder about your lover.

280. You'll receive a gift that makes you wonder: Does this man really know me?

281. You'll buy something extravagant to wear for your lover.

    a. A whole new wardrobe.

    b. A pair of shoes you can barely walk in.

    c. A dress that makes you wonder: Sexy or pushing my luck?

282. You'll buy lingerie.

    a. A black lace teddy.

    b. A fishnet bra and matching bikini.

    c. Bikini underwear with an arrow pointing down.

283. You'll act as if sexy negligees are all you ever wear to bed.

    a. If he only knew.

284. You'll stand in line at Victoria's Secret and glance at the woman in front of you.

285. She'll be young.

    a. Beautiful.

    b. Hopefully wearing a Wonderbra.

    c. Probably not wearing a bra at all.

286. You'll say, "Forty bucks for a bra; he better be Mr. Right."

287. She'll say, "The thongs are on sale."

288. You'll be tempted to buy a thong.

289. You'll realize a thong would show off your finest feature.
   a. If you were seventeen.
   b. If you were a professional volleyball player.

290. You'll tell yourself you're sick of panty-line.

291. You'll tell the saleswoman you're sick of panty-line.

292. The saleswoman will say, "Who is he?"

293. You'll say, "I think he's Mr. Right."

294. You'll discover that thongs come in all shapes and one size.
   a. Not big enough.

295. You'll discover that two thongs still don't make one full pair of underwear.

296. You'll choose two thongs.
a. One medium.
b. One large.

297. You'll feel like you're doing something you shouldn't be doing.

298. You are.

299. It won't be the first time.

300. Your lover will love your sexy underwear.

301. Especially the thong.

302. He won't care that you're not a gymnast.
a. A professional volleyball player.
b. Seventeen.

303. You'll discover that this is one of a man's finest qualities.

304. You'll discover myriad other fine qualities.

305.

306.

I'm thinking . . .

305. The man will love your body.

306. The man will love your mind.

307. The man will love your cooking.

308. You'll think: What's wrong with this man?
    a. This is not one of a woman's finest qualities.

309. You'll wonder why he's still single.

310. You'll wonder about his past lovers.

311. You'll ask him about his last girlfriend.

312. He'll be dumb enough to tell you.

313. You'll be dumb enough to believe him.

314. He'll say, "She was beautiful, smart, funny,
    ambitious, but we were just too young."
    *a. "Her career was more important to her than
      anything. She's a marine biologist."*
    b. "The relationship was all about sex."

315. You will be sorry you asked the man about his ex.

316. Not as sorry as he'll be for telling you about her.

317. You'll harass the man for details about his ex.

318. You'll say, "I thought we'd order in tonight, how long was her long brown hair?"
  a. *"How's the mu shu pork, so do you still talk to her?"*
  b. *"What do you mean—really organized?"*

319. You'll imagine the two of them together.
  a. *At the aquarium.*
  b. *At Bed Bath & Beyond.*
  c. *In bed.*

320. You'll say, "Just what the world needs, another marine biologist."
  a. *"Being organized is great, but I think it's more important to be a decent human being."*
  b. *"My hair was long, before I cut it."*

321. You'll realize you sound like a lunatic.

322. Your man will realize he'd better change the subject.

323. Your man will ask you about *your* ex.

324. You'll say, "His name is Bob."

325. He'll say, "Oh, well, good night, honey."

326. You'll wonder why a woman can't be more like a man.

327. You will ponder this question for about as long as it takes to pee.

328. Then you'll wonder if the lavender soap on his sink ledge was really his idea.

329. You'll wonder what other mementos of his ex he has hidden in his apartment.

330. You'll snoop through the man's apartment.

331. You'll look in his medicine cabinet.

332. You'll look in his underwear drawer.

333. You'll look in his closet.

334. You'll find something you wish you hadn't.
   a. A closet that's neater than your living room.
   b. Twister.
   c. A videotape labeled: Aruba.

335. You'll realize you have three choices.
   a. Invade his privacy further and watch the video.
   b. Respect his privacy.
   c. Call your girlfriend and ask her what she'd do.

336. She'll say, "Do you want a relationship based on mutual trust and respect?"
   a. Normally, this question would be a no-brainer.

337. You'll say, "His ex-girlfriend is a long-haired, really organized marine biologist."

338. She'll say, "What are you waiting for?"

339. You'll decide to act with honesty and integrity.
a. *Most of the time.*
b. *Much of the time.*
c. *Time is relative.*

340. You'll do something that you'll never tell the man you did.
a. *Watch him snorkeling.*
b. *Watch his friends snorkeling.*
c. *Fast-forward to see if there's anything more interesting than a bunch of guys snorkeling.*

341. You'll feel horrible for snooping through the man's apartment.
a. *Okay, bad.*
b. *Okay, kinda bad.*

342. You'll realize that if the man snooped through *your* apartment you'd throw a fit.
a. *Be fit to be tied.*
b. *Die of shame.*

343. You'll consider telling the man what you did.

344. You'll realize that being a decent human being isn't all *that* important.

345. You'll realize there are other ways to show you care—like making dinner.

346. You'll decide to impress the man with your culinary skills.

347. Whether you have them or not will have no bearing.

348. You'll think: Coq au vin, how hard could it be?
   a. Fried chicken, how hard could it be?
   b. Marine biology, four years of school, tops.

349. You'll realize your motives aren't the lofty kind.

350. You won't let that stand in your way, either.

351. You'll be amazed at the results of your culinary efforts.
   a. Total and complete disaster.
   b. 150 dollars' worth of groceries down the drain.
   c. Salad.

352. You'll realize you have three choices.

    a. Cry.

    b. Admit that the man was a fool for breaking up with his ex-girlfriend and hooking up with you.

    c. Drink the wine that was meant for the coq au vin.

353. You'll call your girlfriend drunk and defeated.

354. You'll say, "I'm not Julia Child."

    a. "I'm not a marine biologist."

    b. "I couldn't even get through Moby-Dick."

355. She'll say, "No one can get through *Moby-Dick*."

356. You'll say, "*She* probably did."

357. You'll realize you've reached a new level of lunacy.

358. You'll realize the bottle you're drinking from reads: *For cooking purposes only*.

359. Neither of these revelations will stop you.

360. You'll decide to call the man.

361. Your girlfriend will try to stop you.
  a. Ha.

362. You'll call the man and make a complete
  and total fool of yourself.

363. You'll say something like, "I just don't know
  if you're strong enough to be my man."
  *a. "A marine biologist, like, what, that's supposed
  to make me jealous?"*
  *b. "I'm not like your other girlfriends, I'm
  completely different."*
  *c. "Just so you know, my ex-boyfriend almost
  made the Olympic swimming team."*

364. You'll scare the hell out of the man.

365. You'd scare the hell out of your cat if he hadn't
  discovered your chicken.

366. You'll wake up in the morning feeling like you
  made the biggest mistake of your life.
  a. Oh, if only that were true.

367. You'll wonder how you can possibly save face.

368. You'll ponder your options.

    a. Admit to him that you're jealous and insecure.

    b. Admit to him that every once in a while you go off the deep end.

    c. Admit to him that Mastering the Art of French Cooking was an impulse buy.

    d. Admit that you're in love with him.

369. You'll pick "d."

370. This will be the biggest mistake of your life.

371. You'll learn from it, though.

    a. Not to ever, ever do it again.

    b. Not to do it when the man is reaching for his wineglass.

    c. Not to waste time trying to interpret his response.

372. You'll waste lots of time trying to interpret his response.

373. You'll waste lots of time wondering why he hasn't called.

374. You won't be able to eat.

375. You won't be able to sleep.

376. Sparkling bathroom tile will be a distant memory.

377. You'll pace the floors in the wee hours of the night.

378. For some reason this will entertain your cat.

379. Then you'll call your girlfriend.

380. She'll say, "You just woke me up from a perfect dream."

381. You'll say, "Let me guess, the groom was faceless."
   a. "The dress was Vera Wang."

382. She'll say, "No, the groom was that guy on *CSI,* what's his name?"

383. You'll say, "Well *he's* probably a jerk, too."

384. She'll say, "Oh, God, what happened?"

385. You'll say, "I told him I love him."

386. She'll say, "What did he say?"

387. You'll say, "He said, 'Oh, Jesus, I'm so sorry. Waiter!'"

388. She'll say, "Well, that could mean anything."

389. Then she'll say, "Oh, sweetie, didn't you read *The Rules*?"

390. You'll say, "No, I read *The Second Sex*."

391. She'll say, "You got through *The Second Sex,* and you couldn't get through *Moby-Dick*?"

392. Then she'll say, "Do you want to come over? I'm out of cooking sherry, but I've got vodka."

393. You'll realize you can live without a man but not without your girlfriends.

394. You'll realize you can live without vodka, but so what?

395. You'll spend hours with your girlfriend talking about men.

396. You'll spend hours with your girlfriend talking about women.

397. You will come to one conclusion.
   a. Women are better.

398. You will come to another conclusion.
   a. That if the man knew half of what you tell your girlfriend he'd throw a fit.
   b. Be fit to be tied.
   c. Kill you.

399. You'll sip your drink and say, "What was I saying?"

400. She'll say, "You were telling me about the time he tried to ravish you but his feet got stuck in his jeans and he almost broke his neck."

401. You'll finish telling the story.

402. Your girlfriend will be in stitches.

403. When she gets ahold of herself she'll say, "Maybe he's not a jerk, maybe he's just a klutz."

404. You'll think: My God, Maybe She's Right.

405. You'll think: My God, That Makes Sense.

406. It won't make any sense.

407. For one fleeting moment you'll wonder if you're desperate enough to believe anything.

408. Then you'll say, "What did you say?"

409. Your girlfriend will say, "I said, do you want another drink?"

410. For one fleeting moment you'll wonder if you should have another drink.

411. Then you'll say, "Less ice."

412. When she hands you the glass, you'll say, "I love you, you know."

413. She'll say, "I love you too."

414. You'll both clink glasses.
  a. And neither of you will spill a drop.

415. You'll do three things when you wake up in the morning.
  a. Reschedule your eleven o'clock bikini wax for the following Saturday.
  b. Brush your teeth with your fingers.
  c. Decide to surprise the man who's probably just a klutz.

416. For one fleeting moment you'll wonder if you should call him first.

417. Then you'll think: My God, look at my hair.

418. You'll fix your hair.

419. You'll pick the cat fur off your top.

420. You'll leave a note for your girlfriend:
  Love you. Call me.

421. You'll buy two coffees,
   a. two muffins,
   b. a Star magazine,
      which you'll keep in your car.

422. You'll decide to say something irresistible when
   he opens the door, like: Coffee?
   a. Tea?
   b. Beaujolais Nouveau?

423. You'll smile to yourself thinking about his
   response.

424. You'll giggle to yourself remembering the story
   you told your girlfriend.

425. You'll feel compassion for the man who just
   can't be trusted with stemware.

426. Then you'll stop at his door.

427. You'll toss back your hair,
   a. strike a sexy pose,
   b. knock on his door.

428. A woman will open the door.

429. She'll be young,

    a. beautiful,

    b. hopefully the cleaning lady,

    c. whose long brown hair is mid-shoulder length.

430. She'll say, "So you're the new girlfriend."

431. You'll say, "So you're the marine biologist."

432. She'll say, "Don't worry, I just came to get my things."

433. She'll be holding the Twister.

434. She'll see you holding the coffee.

435. She'll say, "Oh, God, don't tell me—you met him in Starbucks."

436. You'll say, "A quaint little café."

437. She'll say, "Whatever. Did he tell you he loves you?"

438. You'll say, "Not exactly."

439. She'll say, "He lies."

440. Then she'll say, "I bet he told you he loves Russian authors."

441. You'll nod.

442. She'll say, "He couldn't even get through *Moby-Dick*."

443. Then she'll notice the cat fur on your top.

444. She'll say, "Oh, God, don't tell me—he told you he loves cats."

445. You'll say, "He doesn't love cats?"

446. She'll say, "He hates them."

447. Then she'll say, "You know, I really thought he was Mr. Right. Turns out he's just a jerk."

448. She'll glance at the coffee.

449. You'll hand her one.

450. She'll say, "Thanks," hand you the man's key, and close the door behind her.

451. As she walks away you'll say, "Nobody gets through *Moby-Dick*!"

452. She'll stop, look over her shoulder, and say, "Are you sure?"

453. You won't be sure.

454. Suddenly, you won't be sure about anything.

455. You'll leave the man's place and walk back to your car.

456. Suddenly, you'll be sure of one thing.

457. You locked your keys in your car.

458. You'll realize you have two choices.
a. Cry.
b. Bang your fists on the car and shout obscenities.

459. You'll pick "a."

460. When you pull yourself together you'll think: No man is going to make a fool out of me.

   a. No man is going to get the best of me.

   b. This is an emergency.

461. You'll call the man to rescue you.

   a. Nine times out of ten an emergency will have something to do with your car.

462. The man will come to your rescue.

463. You'll be touched by his kindness,

   a. Moved by his courage in the face of not having the slightest idea what he's doing.

   b. Overcome by desire watching him manhandle your power windows.

464. You'll discover a cold, harsh truth about yourself: It doesn't take much.

465. Then he'll wipe the sweat from his brow,

   a. hand you your keys,

   b. and say, "Your oil is low. Your transmission fluid could use a change. Are you hungry?"

466. You'll be starved.

467. He'll take you to a quaint, neighborhood Italian place.

468. He'll lead you to a little corner table.

469. He'll order a bottle of Chianti.

470. Suddenly, the ex-girlfriend will seem really insignificant.

471. Suddenly, literacy will seem really overrated.

472. Suddenly, nothing in the world will matter except you and him and the olives he's feeding you with his fingers.

473. He'll gaze at you, knowingly.

474. You'll gaze back at him, knowingly.

475. Then he'll say, "There's something I've been meaning to ask you . . ."

476. You'll think: Yes, I'd like to be married someday.

    a. Yes, I think about having kids.

    b. Yes, I'd be willing to take a cooking class, organize my closet, lose ten pounds.

477. He'll say, "How's Fluffy?"

478. You'll say, "How's *Fluffy?*"

479. He'll say, "Yeah, you said he got sick from something he ate."

480. You'll say, "Yeah. Bad fish."

481. He'll say, "I thought it was coq au vin."

482. You'll say, "What do you care, you don't even like cats!"

483. He'll say, "What do you mean? I think cats are great."

484. You'll say, "Do you love them?"

485. He'll say, "Cats?"

486. You'll say, "Yes, cats!"

487. He'll say, "What kind of a question is that?"

488. You'll say, "It's a simple question—yes or no? Do You Love Cats?"

489. The man's silence will tell you everything.
   a. Okay, not quite everything.

490. The bartender will wander over to your table.

491. She'll be young.
   a. Beautiful.
   b. Auditioning in the morning for a part in an edgy thriller.

492. She'll say to you, "It was just one night, okay? He doesn't love me."

493. You'll say, "Who the hell are you?"

494. She'll say, "I'm Cat."

495. Then she'll say to him, "I can't believe you told her. God, what a jerk."

496. A man will break your heart.

    a. Oh, let me count the ways.

    b. Oh, at least once, another woman will be the way.

497. You will not succumb to tears.

498. You will not succumb to lunacy.

499. You will not succumb to picking up the butter knife and plunging it into your heart.

    a. All that will come later.

500. You will look at the man who moments ago had his fingers in your mouth and ask him the eternal question:

    a. "Why?"

501. And the man will look back at you and respond with the eternal answer:

    a. "I dunno."

502. And with that you will get up and walk out of his life forever.

503. Thirty seconds into forever you'll change your mind.

504. Then you'll succumb to lunacy.

505. You'll be amazed at the result of your psychotic outburst.
   a. Total and complete attention from restaurant patrons.
   b. Total and complete attention from restaurant staff.
   c. A little satisfaction.

506. Then you'll do what any strong, independent woman would do who just screamed, "And just so you know, you're *not* the first man I've slept with who could play 'Stairway to Heaven' on the guitar!"
   a. Walk out of the restaurant. Forever.

507. Then you'll go home and succumb to tears.
   a. For some reason your cat will understand and curl up in your lap.

508. You'll do three things when you wake up in the morning.
a. Push your cat off your face.
b. Remove your coat and boots.
c. Call your girlfriend.

509. She'll say one word that will send you spiraling into the depths of despair.
a. "Hello?"

510. Then she'll say, "I'll be right over."

511. Your girlfriend will try to comfort you.

512. Your girlfriend will try to console you.

513. After three weeks she'll be sick of you.

514. After three weeks your coworkers will be sick of you.

515. *You* will just be getting started.

516. You'll rip up all his pictures.

517. You'll burn all his poems.

518. You'll call your girlfriend and say, "Listen to this . . . 'I lay awake at night, thinking of you.'"

519. She'll say, "Uh-huh . . . "

520. You'll say, "It's *lie,* 'I *lie* awake'—God, what an idiot. Can you believe what an idiot he is?"

521. Your girlfriend will not say, "Sweetie, you've gone off the deep end."

522. Your girlfriend will not say, "Sweetie, nobody knows when to use *lie* and when to use *lay*."

523. She *will* say, "Sweetie, why don't you make yourself a nice cup of tea and watch some *CSI*."

524. You'll take her advice.

525. Then you'll imagine standing next to a cute CSI as he uncovers the dead body of your ex and saying, "Yep, that's him."

526. Then the cute CSI will say, "He looks kinda like Liam Neeson."

527. And you'll say, "*Looked*. He looked *kinda* like Liam Neeson. Such a shame."

528. You'll lie awake, night after night, watching movies like *Betrayal*.
   a. Damage.
   b. When Harry Met Sally . . . .

529. You'll lie around, weekend after weekend, watching shows like *E! True Hollywood Story.*
   a. The Fabulous Life of . . . .
   b. Iron Chef.

530. You'll realize you don't need anything but your cat.
   a. Your television.
   b. Phone numbers for restaurants that deliver.

531. You'll realize it's okay to let a few things fall by the wayside.
   a. Like shaving your legs.
   b. Taking out the garbage.
   c. Getting dressed.

532. Then one day, as you're putting Jelly Bellys into color-coordinated piles, there will be a knock on your door.

533. Your first thought will be: It's the police.

534. Your second thought will be: I've been watching too much *CSI*.

535. Your third thought will be: It's Him.
   a. No, not Him, the Almighty, you won't be that crazy. But Him—the man who broke your heart.

536. You'll walk to the door,
   a. pull the scrunchie from your hair,
   b. and strike as sexy a pose as you can in sweatpants and a Grateful Dead T-shirt.

537. Then you'll open the door.

538. It'll be your girlfriend.

539. She'll walk in and see the empty Chinese food containers.

    a. The cookie dough roll with a spoon stuck in it.

    b. The cat, who's never looked happier, on top of a mountain of dirty laundry.

540. She'll say, "Put the jelly beans down."

    a. "Get dressed."

    b. "We're going shopping."

541. You'll say, "I'm not ready to go shopping."

542. She'll say, "Barneys is having a sale."

543. You'll say, "I think it's time I got on with my life."

544. You'll find the strength to get on with your life.

    a. Somehow.

545. You'll find your credit card still has room on it.

    a. Somehow.

546. Before you know it, you'll be over him.
   a. Practically.

547. You'll do a few things when you're
   practically over him.
   a. Shave.
   b. Pluck.
   c. Manicure.
   d. Pedicure.
   e. Take yoga.
   f. Listen to Sinéad O'Connor.
   g. Organize your closet listening to Sinéad O'Connor.

548. Then one day you'll realize you're Out There
   Again.

549. You'll realize you're Out There Again because
   a recently married college friend you run into
   at Bed Bath & Beyond will say, "Jeez, I can't
   imagine being Out There Again."

550. You'll say, "It's really not that bad."
   a. "I enjoy being single."
   *b. "I really don't have time for a man, now that
      I'm back in school."*

551. She'll say, "Oh, you're back in school. What for?"

552. You'll say, "Law."

553. She'll say, "Law. Wow. Weren't you a poetry major?"

554. You'll say, "Well, people change."

555. You'll decide it's perfectly acceptable to lie to old college friends.

556. Then she'll say, "It's a shame you're so busy. My husband has a friend."
   a. "He's single."
   b. "Cute."
   c. "Just made partner in his law firm."

557. For one fleeting moment you'll wonder if you're desperate enough to go on a blind date.
   a. Rule of thumb: If you're desperate enough to take yoga, you're desperate enough to go on a blind date.

558. You'll say, "It's not like I study *all* the time."

559. She'll say, "Great, I'll have him call you."

560. You'll say, "Great. Nice sheets, by the way."

561. Then you'll go home, find a butter knife, and
plunge it into your heart.
a. I'm kidding.

562. You'll go home and call your girlfriend.

563. You'll say, "Do you think I'm desperate
enough to go on a blind date?"

564. She'll say, "What did you rent from
Blockbuster?"

565. You'll say, "*9½ Weeks*."

566. She'll say, "Yes."

567. You'll thank her and tell her you'll call her
when your blind date calls.

568. He won't call.
a. After 9½ Weeks.
b. After 2½ hours after 9½ Weeks.
*c. After 2½ hours after 9½ Weeks and a
three-minute microwave meal.*

569. You'll forget you wondered if you were desperate enough to go on a blind date and wonder desperately why the jerk hasn't called you.

570. Then the phone will ring.

571. You'll trip over your cat hurrying to answer it.

572. It'll be the man who broke your heart.

573. He'll say something irresistible like, "Hi."

574. A voice inside your head will scream: Hang up the phone!

575. It'll be the same voice that screams: Get out of the cookie aisle!

576. You won't listen to that voice.

577. You'll listen to old faithful.
   a. Yep, your heart.

578. Then he'll say, "What are you doing?"

579. You'll say, "I was about to take a bath. Naked. But what do you care?"

580. The voice will have nothing more to say to you.

581. The man will say, "I do still care."

582. You will believe him.
   a. Why?
   b. For the same reason you believed Barneys was having a sale.

583. You'll agree to meet the man who broke your heart.

584. You'll feel like you're doing something you shouldn't be doing.

585. Therefore, you won't tell anyone.

586. You'll meet him at a quaint little Irish pub.
   a. Dressed to kill.

587. He'll be seated at the end of the bar.
   a. Dressed in Hugo Boss and sporting a goatee.

588. Rod Stewart's "Da Ya Think I'm Sexy?" will start playing from the jukebox.
   a. I'm not kidding.

589. Suddenly, nothing in the world will matter except you and him and the scotch that's on the way.

590. One drink will turn into two.

591. Two drinks will turn into three.

592. Three drinks will turn into something you will definitely not tell anyone.

593. You'll wake up the next morning and push your cat off your face.
a. There will be no cat on your face.

594. The phone will ring.

595. It'll be your girlfriend.

596. You'll say, "Oh, God, you're never going to believe what I did last night."

597. She'll say, "You went out with the man and got drunk."

598. You'll say, "Yep."

599. She'll say, "Did anything else happen?"

600. You'll say, "Yep."

601. She'll say, "Oh, God, you didn't . . . "

602. You'll say, "Nope."

603. She'll say, "So, what happened?"

604. You'll say, "We slow danced to 'My Eyes Adored You.'"
   a. "We made out in the parking lot."
   b. "I told him I still loved him."

605. She'll say, "Oh, God, that's worse than . . . "

606. You'll say, "I know, I know."

607. Then she'll say, "What did he say?"

608. You'll say, "He said, 'That's cool. Do you have my Smashing Pumpkins CD? I can't find it anywhere.'"

609. She'll say, "Oh, sweetie, I'm so sorry."

610. You'll say, "It's okay, I learned from it."

611. She'll say, "What did you learn?"

612. You'll say, "That scotch isn't my drink."

613. Your girlfriend will chuckle.

614. You'll realize you still have your sense
of humor.
a. Somehow.

615. And with your sense of humor firmly intact
you will agree to a blind date.

616. Your first thought will be: I wonder what he
looks like.

617. Your second thought will be: I wonder what he
looks like.

618. Your third thought will be:
I wonder if there's any milk in the
fridge. Frosted Flakes sound good.

619. Your blind date will look nothing like you imagined.

    a. (Handsome actor in Law and Order series.)

620. Your blind date will not be as witty and charming as you imagined.

    a. Conversation will turn to his food allergies: wheat, yeast, dairy, gluten.

621. You'll sip your wine and say, "Gluten? What's gluten?"

    a. Conversation will turn to the subject of gluten.

622. You'll still give your blind date a chance.

    a. Why?

    b. Desperation.

    c. The waiter is kind of cute.

623. Then he'll kiss you good night.

    a. No, not the waiter, your insufferable blind date.

624. His kiss will be exactly like you imagined.

    a. Garlic—not something he's allergic to.

625. Your girlfriend will call. She'll say, "How was your blind date?"

626. You'll say, "Oh, God, you'll never believe what he talked about over dinner."

627. She'll say, "His BMW?"

628. You'll say, "No, gluten."

629. She'll say, "I hate when men talk about gluten. What's gluten?"

630. You'll say, "It's the part of the wheat . . . Oh, God, I'm never going on a date ever again."

631. She'll say, "Your ex called me."

632. You'll say, "My ex called you? Oh, my God, what did he say?"

633. She'll say, "Not that ex. Your other ex."

634. You'll say, "My other ex? He moved to Tucson—why on earth would *he* call you?"

635. She'll say, "Not that ex. Your other ex."

636. You'll say, "Okay, would you just cut to the chase and tell me which of my exes called you?"

637. She'll say, "The one who was living with that French model."

638. You'll say, "*Was?*"

639. She'll say, "Yep."

640. Then you'll say, "Why on earth would *he* call you?"

641. She'll say, "He wanted to know if you were seeing anyone."

642. You'll say, "What did you say?"

643. Then you'll say, "Okay, what did he say when you told him I wasn't seeing anyone?"

644. She'll say, "He wanted to know if I thought you'd be interested . . . in seeing him again."

645. You'll say, "And What Did You Say?"

646. She'll say, "I told him you'd be interested in seeing *anyone*."

647. You'll realize your girlfriend still has her sense of humor—and you don't appreciate it.

648. Then you'll say, "Do you think I should call him?"

649. She'll say, "What did you rent from Blockbuster?"

650. You'll say, "*An Affair to Remember.*"

651. She'll say, "Was it?"

652. You'll say, "Was it what?"

653. She'll say, "An affair to remember?"

654. You'll say, "I don't remember."

655. Then you'll say, "Oh, God, I do remember this one night . . ."

656. She'll say, "Yes, I think you should call him."

657. You will call an old flame.

658. You'll meet him at a romantic restaurant.

659. He'll say, "You smell so good."

660. You'll say, "It's Chanel N°5."

661. He'll say, "I ordered red."

662. You'll say, "You know me well."

663. Then he'll say, "Do you remember that one night . . . "

664. You'll say, "How could I forget?"

665. Everything Will Be Perfect.

666. Then you'll say, "So, tell me, what happened with you and Claudette?"
a. Why will you say this?
b. So far, experts only have theories.

667. He'll tell you about Claudette over escargots.

668. He'll tell you about Claudette over chateaubriand.

669. He'll tell you about Claudette over crème brûlée.

670. You will be sorry you asked about Claudette.

671. Then, as he's walking you to your doorstep, he'll say, "So, tell me, what happened with you and that guy who looked like Liam Neeson?"

672. You'll say, "He cheated on me with a woman named Cat."

673. He'll say, "Claudette's mother's name is Cat."

674. You'll say, "Oh. Well, good night."

675. You'll go upstairs and call your girlfriend. You'll say, "You wanna get a beer?"

676. She'll say, "How was your date?"

677. You'll say, "You wanna get several beers?"

678. Then you'll say, "He spent the entire evening talking about his ex. How was your date?"

679. She'll say, "He spent the entire evening talking about his screenplay."

680. You'll say, "Oh, God, that's worse."

681. She'll say, "I know."

682. Then she'll say, "I'd love to get a beer."

683. You'll go out with your girlfriend.
   a. With no thoughts of meeting Mr. Right.
   b. With a fleeting thought of meeting Mr. Right.
   c. Dressed to kill just in case.

684. You'll be older,
   a. wiser,
   b. more discerning.
   c. Okay, older.

685. You'll discover all the men in the bar are Younger.

686. You'll join a health club hoping to meet Mr. Right.

687. You'll discover all the men in the health club are Bigger And Dumber.

688. You'll go to the grocery store for Häagen-Dazs—oh, and hoping to meet Mr. Right.

689. You'll discover all the men in the grocery store are Married And Shopping For Their Wives.
   a. Single And Shopping For Miller Genuine Draft.

690. You'll go to a bowling alley hoping to meet Mr. Right.

691. You'll discover all the men in the bowling alley are Men You'd Expect To Meet In A Bowling Alley.

692. You'll wonder where to meet a man.

693. You'll discover Nobody Knows.

694. You'll go home and call your mother.

695. You'll discover Nobody Knows—except your mother.

696. She'll remind you about your cousin's wedding.

697. She'll remind you that the groom's best man is available.

698. She'll remind you that you're thirty-five.

699. You'll say, "Mom, I'm thirty-*three*."

700. She'll say, "There's still hope."

701. You'll go to a wedding hoping to meet Mr. Right.

702. You'll discover all the women at the wedding are Thirty-Three And Hoping To Meet Mr. Right.

703. You'll go to the bar hoping the bartender knows how to make a Manhattan straight up.

704. The bartender will fix you a drink.

705. He'll be young.

    a. Cute.

    b. Way too young and way too cute.

706. This won't stop you.

    a. Why?

    b. A number of reasons, like: You haven't had sex in eight months. You haven't had sex in eight months. You haven't had sex in eight months.

707. You'll have a fling.

708. You'll feel like you're doing something you shouldn't be doing.

709. Therefore, you'll tell everyone.

    a. Except your mother.

710. You'll realize you really *don't* need a man, you just need sex.

    a. I'm kidding.

    b. Sort of kidding.

711. Then one day you'll realize you want more than a fling.

712. You'll realize you want True Love.

713. You'll discover a cold, harsh truth about yourself: You're not a realist.

714. You'll decide true love is worth the wait.

715. You'll wait.
   a. For as long as it takes.
   b. Longer than you intended.

716. You'll have a long, dry spell.

717. You'll do a few things during your long, dry spell.
   a. Catch up on your reading.
   b. Catch up with old friends.
   c. Scrub your tile.
   d. Bake bread.
   e. Try to bake bread and wonder how anyone can bake bread.

718. Then one day you'll realize you *are* thirty-five.
   a. And still single.
   b. And still unable to fit into your skinny jeans.
   c. And watching season two of Friends.

719. You'll realize you have two choices.

    a. Accept your age with dignity and grace.

    b. Drastic measures.

720. You'll pick "b."

721. You'll consider the drastic measures.

    a. Club Med for singles.

    b. Match.com.

    c. Calling your mother.

722. You'll pick "c."

723. She'll tell you that there's still hope.

724. You will believe her.

    a. Why?

    b. Because she's your mother.

725. Then she'll say, "My friend has a son—he's a doctor."

    a. "Lawyer."

    b. "He'd be perfect for you."

726. You'll say, "Mom, I went on a blind date once and the man spent the entire evening talking about gluten."

727. She'll say, "Was he Jewish?"

728. Then she'll say, "Why don't you stop by today? I baked some bread."

729. You will be sorry you called your mother.

730. You'll say, "I have some errands to run. I'll call you later."

731. You won't have any errands to run.

732. You won't have anything left to clean.
  a. Except your closet.
  b. Which doesn't count.

733. You'll call your girlfriend.

734. She won't be home.

735. Suddenly, you'll realize you have nothing to do.
a. Except shop.
b. Which counts.

736. You'll go out by yourself.
a. With no thoughts of meeting Mr. Right.
b. With a fleeting thought of needing a new bathing suit for Club Med for singles.
c. With a fleeting thought of needing a new shower curtain lining.

737. You'll wander into Barneys.

738. You'll wander into Bed Bath & Beyond.

739. Suddenly, you'll realize you don't feel like shopping.
a. I'm not kidding.

740. Then you'll wander by a pet store.

741. You'll stop and look in the window.

742. You'll look at the cute, furry bunnies.

743. You'll look at the cute, furry puppies.

744. You'll look at the iguana.

745. You'll wonder why anyone would want to own an iguana.

746. Then you'll see a cat.

747. He'll be fat,
a. happy,
b. and playing with a catnip-stuffed mouse.

748. You'll realize your cat doesn't have a catnip-stuffed mouse.

749. Suddenly, you'll feel like shopping.
a. Like I said, it doesn't take much.

750. You'll wander into the pet store.

751. You'll ignore the tropical fish.

752. You'll ignore the turtles.

753. You'll think the salamanders are cute, but still—a really weird pet.

754. Then, suddenly, you'll see something you can't ignore.
   a. Yep, the kittens.

755. You'll wander over to the kittens.

756. Suddenly, your heart will melt.

757. You'll hold two of the kittens.
   a. One black.
   b. One white.

758. Suddenly, you'll be tempted to buy two kittens.

759. You'll realize if you bought two kittens you'd have three cats.

760. You'll realize if you bought two kittens you'll have officially gone off the deep end.

761. Then, suddenly, you'll notice a man standing next to you.

762. He'll say, "Hard to resist."

763. You'll look at the man.

764. He'll smile.

    a. Yep—hard to resist.

765. Then he'll look at the kittens.

766. He'll say, "May I?"

767. You'll hand him a kitten.

768. You'll see his big, strong hands holding the little, furry kitten.

769. You'll think: Yes, I'd like to be married. Tomorrow.

    a. Yes, I think about having kids. Five or six.

    b. Yes, I'd love to get a cup of coffee.

770. Then he'll say, "Every time I come in here, I have to remind myself that I already have pets."

771. You'll say, "Oh, you have pets. What kind?"

772. He'll say, "Two dogs."

773. For one fleeting moment your heart will sink.

774. Then you'll think: Nobody's perfect.

775. Then he'll say, "I'd love to have a big house someday—with lots of animals."

776. You'll think: Nobody's perfect—except this guy.

777. He'll smile at you again.

778. You'll smile back.

779. Then he'll say, "Would you like to get a cup of coffee?"

780. You'll say, "I'd love to."

781. You'll discover, eventually, that he's not perfect.
  a. *After three cups of coffee.*
  b. *After six months of dating.*
  c. *Lost in Barbados on your honeymoon because the man won't stop to ask for directions.*
  d. *But that's another book.*

♥